23c 2/09 $^{10}/98$

only copy

CREATIVE CLASSICS

This wonderful short story
has passed the test of a classic:
it has lasted.
Our eyes still race eagerly as its characters
face danger, confusion or sadness.
The experience becomes a reservoir of strength.
It lies quiet in our memories until
we need a deeper wisdom
to face our own danger, confusion or sadness.
This story,
like others in the Creative Classic series,
has been rescued from the
musty, attic-world of anthologies.
It is here presented in a volume of its own,
with all the richness and dignity
a good story deserves.

ISAAC ASIMOV

Robbie

with illustrations by
David Shannon

CREATIVE EDUCATION, INC

MANKATO, MINNESOTA

Published by Creative Education, Inc.
123 South Broad Street, Mankato, Minnesota 56001

Printed in the United States of America.
ISBN 0-88682-231-9

To Janet,
who's made a storybook
of my life

Ninety-eight—ninety-nine—one hundred." Gloria withdrew her chubby little forearm from before her eyes and stood for a moment, wrinkling her nose and blinking in the sunlight. Then, trying to watch in all directions at once, she withdrew a few cautious steps from the tree against which she had been leaning.

She craned her neck to investigate the possibilities of a clump of bushes to the right and then withdrew farther to obtain a better angle for viewing its dark recesses. The quiet was profound except for the incessant buzzing of insects and the occasional chirrup of some hardy bird, braving the midday sun.

Gloria pouted, "I bet he went inside the house, and I've told him a million times that that's not fair."

With tiny lips pressed together tightly and a severe frown crinkling her forehead, she moved determinedly toward the two-story building up past the driveway.

Too late she heard the rustling sound behind her, followed by the distinctive and rhythmic clump-clump of Robbie's metal feet. She whirled about to see her triumphing companion emerge from hiding and make for the home-tree at full speed.

Gloria shrieked in dismay. "Wait, Robbie! That wasn't fair, Robbie! You promised you wouldn't run until I found you." Her little feet could make no headway at all against Robbie's giant strides. Then, within ten feet of the goal, Robbie's pace slowed suddenly to the merest of crawls, and Gloria, with one final burst of wild speed, dashed pantingly past him to touch the welcome bark of home-tree first.

Gleefully, she turned on the faithful Robbie, and with the basest of ingratitude, rewarded him for his sacrifice by taunting him cruelly for a lack of running ability.

"Robbie can't run," she shouted at the top of her eight-year-old voice. "I can beat him any day. I can beat him any day." She chanted the words in a shrill rhythm.

Robbie didn't answer, of course—not in words. He pantomimed running instead, inching away until Gloria found herself running after him as he dodged her narrowly, forcing her to veer in helpless circles, little arms outstretched and fanning at the air.

"Robbie," she squealed, "stand still!"—And the laughter was forced out of her in breathless jerks.

—Until he turned suddenly and caught her up, whirling her round, so that for her the world fell away for a moment with a blue emptiness beneath, and green trees stretching hungrily downward toward the void. Then she was down in the grass again, leaning against Robbie's leg and still holding a hard, metal finger.

After a while, her breath returned. She pushed uselessly at her disheveled hair in vague imitation of one of her mother's gestures and twisted to see if her dress were torn.

She slapped her hand against Robbie's torso, "Bad boy! I'll spank you!"

And Robbie cowered, holding his hands over his face so that she had to add, "No, I won't, Robbie. I won't spank you. But anyway, it's my turn to hide now because you've got longer legs and you promised not to run till I found you."

Robbie nodded his head—a small parallelepiped with rounded edges and corners attached to a similar but much larger parallelepiped that served as torso by means of a short, flexible stalk—and obediently faced the tree. A thin, metal film descended over his glowing eyes and from within his body came a steady, resonant ticking.

"Don't peek now—and don't skip any numbers," warned Gloria, and scurried for cover.

With unvarying regularity, seconds were ticked off, and at the hundredth, up went the eyelids, and the glowing red of Robbie's eyes swept the prospect. They rested for a moment on a bit of colorful gingham that protruded from behind a boulder. He advanced a few steps and convinced himself that it was Gloria who squatted behind it.

Slowly, remaining always between Gloria and home-tree, he advanced on the hiding place, and when Gloria was plainly in sight and could no longer even theorize to herself that she was not seen, he extended one arm toward her, slapping the other against his leg so that it rang again. Gloria emerged sulkily.

"You peeked!" she exclaimed, with gross unfairness. "Besides I'm tired of playing hide-and-seek. I want a ride."

But Robbie was hurt at the unjust accusation, so he seated himself carefully and shook his head ponderously from side to side.

Gloria changed her tone to one of gentle coaxing immediately, "Come on, Robbie. I didn't mean it about the peeking. Give me a ride."

Robbie was not to be won over so easily, though. He gazed stubbornly at the sky, and shook his head even more emphatically.

"Please, Robbie, please give me a ride." She encircled his neck with rosy arms and hugged tightly. Then, changing moods in a moment, she moved away. "If you don't, I'm going to cry," and her face twisted appallingly in preparation.

Hard-hearted Robbie paid scant attention to this dreadful possibility, and shook his head a third time. Gloria found it necessary to play her trump card.

"If you don't," she exclaimed warmly, "I won't tell you any more stories, that's all. Not one—"

Robbie gave in immediately and unconditionally before this ultimatum, nodding his head vigorously until the metal of his neck hummed. Carefully, he raised the little girl and placed her on his broad, flat shoulders.

Gloria's threatened tears vanished immediately and she crowed with delight. Robbie's metal skin, kept at a constant temperature of seventy by the high resistance coils within, felt nice and comfortable, while the beautifully loud sound her heels made as they bumped rhythmically against his chest was enchanting.

"You're an air-coaster, Robbie, you're a big, silver air-coaster. Hold out your arms straight.—You *got* to, Robbie, if you're going to be an air-coaster."

The logic was irrefutable. Robbie's arms were wings catching the air currents and he was a silver 'coaster.

Gloria twisted the robot's head and leaned to the right. He banked sharply. Gloria equipped the 'coaster with a motor that went "Br-r-r" and then with weapons that went "Powie" and "Sh-sh-shshsh." Pirates were giving chase and the ship's blasters were coming into play. The pirates dropped in a steady rain.

"Got another one.—Two more," she cried.

Then "Faster, men," Gloria said pompously, "we're running out of ammunition." She aimed over her shoulder

with undaunted courage and Robbie was a blunt-nosed spaceship zooming through the void at maximum acceleration.

Clear across the field he sped, to the patch of tall grass on the other side, where he stopped with a suddenness that evoked a shriek from his flushed rider, and then tumbled her onto the soft, green carpet.

Gloria gasped and panted, and gave voice to intermittent whispered exclamations of "That was *nice!*"

Robbie waited until she had caught her breath and then pulled gently at a lock of hair.

"You want something?" said Gloria, eyes wide in an apparently artless complexity that fooled her huge "nursemaid" not at all. He pulled the curl harder.

"Oh, I know. You want a story."

Robbie nodded rapidly.

"Which one?"

Robbie made a semi-circle in the air with one finger.

The little girl protested, "*Again?* I've told you Cinderella a million times. Aren't you tired of it?—It's for babies."

Another semi-circle.

"Oh, well," Gloria composed herself, ran over the details of the tale in her mind (together with her own elaborations, of which she had several) and began:

"Are you ready? Well—once upon a time there was a beautiful little girl whose name was Ella. And she had a terribly cruel step-mother and two very ugly and *very* cruel step-sisters and—"

Gloria was reaching the very climax of the tale—midnight was striking and everything was changing back to the shabby originals lickety-split, while Robbie listened tensely with burning eyes—when the interruption came.

"Gloria!"

It was the high-pitched sound of a woman who has been calling not once, but several times; and had the nervous tone of one in whom anxiety was beginning to overcome impatience.

"Mamma's calling me," said Gloria, not quite happily. "You'd better carry me back to the house, Robbie."

Robbie obeyed with alacrity for somehow there was that in him which judged it best to obey Mrs. Weston, without as much as a scrap of hesitation. Gloria's father was rarely home in the daytime except on Sunday—today, for instance—and when he was, he proved a genial and understanding person. Gloria's mother, however, was a source of uneasiness to Robbie and there was always the impulse to sneak away from her sight.

Mrs. Weston caught sight of them the minute they rose above the masking tufts of long grass and retired inside the house to wait.

"I've shouted myself hoarse, Gloria," she said, severely. "Where were you?"

"I was with Robbie," quavered Gloria. "I was telling him Cinderella, and I forgot it was dinner-time."

"Well, it's a pity Robbie forgot, too." Then, as if that reminded her of the robot's presence, she whirled upon him. "You may go, Robbie. She doesn't need you now." Then, brutally, "And don't come back till I call you."

Robbie turned to go, but hesitated as Gloria cried out in his defense, "Wait, Mamma, you got to let him stay. I didn't finish Cinderella for him. I said I would tell him Cinderella and I'm not finished."

"Gloria!"

"Honest and truly, Mamma, he'll stay so quiet, you won't even know he's here. He can sit on the chair in the corner, and he won't say a word,—I mean he won't *do* anything. Will you, Robbie?"

Robbie, appealed to, nodded his massive head up and down once.

"Gloria, if you don't stop this at once, you shan't see Robbie for a whole week."

The girl's eyes fell. "All right! But Cinderella is his favorite story and I didn't finish it.—And he likes it so much."

The robot left with a disconsolate step and Gloria choked back a sob.

George Weston was comfortable. It was a habit of his to be comfortable on Sunday afternoons. A good, hearty dinner below the hatches; a nice, soft, dilapidated couch on which to sprawl; a copy of the *Times*; slippered feet and shirtless chest;—how could anyone *help* but be comfortable?

He wasn't pleased, therefore, when his wife walked in. After ten years of married life, he still was so unutterably foolish as to love her, and there was no question that he was always glad to see her—still Sunday afternoons just after dinner were sacred to him and his idea of solid com-

fort was to be left in utter solitude for two or three hours. Consequently, he fixed his eye firmly upon the latest reports of the Lefebre-Yoshida expedition to Mars (this one was to take off from Lunar Base and might actually succeed) and pretended she wasn't there.

Mrs. Weston waited patiently for two minutes, then impatiently for two more, and finally broke the silence.

"George!"

"Hmpph?"

"George, I say! *Will* you put down that paper and look at me?"

The paper rustled to the floor and Weston turned a weary face toward his wife, "What is it, dear?"

"You know what it is, George. It's Gloria and that terrible machine."

"What terrible machine?"

"Now don't pretend you don't know what I'm talking about. It's that robot Gloria calls Robbie. He doesn't leave her for a moment."

"Well, why should he? He's not supposed to. And he certainly isn't a terrible machine. He's the best darn robot money can buy and I'm damned sure he set me back half a year's income. He's worth it, though—darn sight cleverer than half my office staff."

He made a move to pick up the paper again, but his wife was quicker and snatched it away.

"You listen to *me*, George. I won't have my daughter entrusted to a machine—and I don't care how clever it is. It has no soul, and no one knows what it may be thinking. A child just isn't *made* to be guarded by a thing of metal."

Weston frowned, "When did you decide this? He's been with Gloria two years now and I haven't seen you worry till now."

"It was different at first. It was a novelty; it took a load off me, and—and it was a fashionable thing to do. But now I don't know. The neighbors—"

"Well, what have the neighbors to do with it. Now, look. A robot is infinitely more to be trusted than a human nursemaid. Robbie was constructed for only one purpose really—to be the companion of a little child. His entire 'mentality' has been created for the purpose. He just can't help being faithful and loving and kind. He's a machine— *made so*. That's more than you can say for humans."

"But something might go wrong. Some—some—" Mrs. Weston was a bit hazy about the insides of a robot, "some little jigger will come loose and the awful thing will go berserk and—and—" She couldn't bring herself to complete the quite obvious thought.

"Nonsense," Weston denied, with an involuntary nervous shiver. "That's completely ridiculous. We had a long discussion at the time we bought Robbie about the First Law of Robotics. You *know* that it is impossible for a robot to harm a human being; that long before enough can go wrong to alter that First Law, a robot would be completely inoperable. It's a mathematical impossibility. Besides I have an engineer from U. S. Robots here twice a year to give the poor gadget a complete overhaul. Why, there's no more chance of anything at all going wrong with Robbie than there is of you or I suddenly going looney—considerably less, in fact. Besides, how are you going to take him away from Gloria?"

He made another futile stab at the paper and his wife tossed it angrily into the next room.

"That's just it, George! She won't play with anyone else. There are dozens of little boys and girls that she should make friends with, but she won't. She won't go *near* them unless I make her. That's no way for a little girl to grow up. You want her to be normal, don't you? You want her to be able to take her part in society."

"You're jumping at shadows, Grace. Pretend Robbie's a dog. I've seen hundreds of children who would rather have their dog than their father."

"A dog is different, George. We *must* get rid of that horrible thing. You can sell it back to the company. I've asked, and you can."

"You've *asked*? Now look here, Grace, let's not go off the deep end. We're keeping the robot until Gloria is older and I don't want the subject brought up again." And with that he walked out of the room in a huff.

Mrs. Weston met her husband at the door two evenings later. "You'll have to listen to this, George. There's bad feeling in the village."

"About what?" asked Weston. He stepped into the washroom and drowned out any possible answer by the splash of water.

Mrs. Weston waited. She said, "About Robbie."

Weston stepped out, towel in hand, face red and angry, "What are you talking about?"

"Oh, it's been building up and building up. I've tried to close my eyes to it, but I'm not going to any more. Most of the villagers consider Robbie dangerous. Children aren't allowed to go near our place in the evenings."

"We trust *our* child with the thing."

"Well, people aren't reasonable about these things."

"Then to hell with them."

"Saying that doesn't solve the problem. I've got to do my shopping down there. I've got to meet them every day. And it's even worse in the city these days when it comes to robots. New York has just passed an ordinance keeping all robots off the streets between sunset and sunrise."

"All right, but they can't stop us from keeping a robot in our home.—Grace, this is one of your campaigns. I recognize it. But it's no use. The answer is still, no! We're keeping Robbie!"

And yet he loved his wife—and what was worse, his wife knew it. George Weston, after all, was only a man—poor thing—and his wife made full use of every device which a clumsier and more scrupulous sex has learned, with reason and futility, to fear.

Ten times in the ensuing week, he cried, "Robbie stays,—and that's *final*!" and each time it was weaker and accompanied by a louder and more agonized groan.

Came the day at last, when Weston approached his daughter guiltily and suggested a "beautiful" visivox show in the village.

Gloria clapped her hands happily, "Can Robbie go?"

"No, dear." he said, and winced at the sound of his voice, "they won't allow robots at the visivox—but you can tell him all about it when you get home." He stumbled all over the last few words and looked away.

Gloria came back from town bubbling over with enthusiasm, for the visivox had been a gorgeous spectacle indeed.

She waited for her father to maneuver the jet-car into the sunken garage, "Wait till I tell Robbie, Daddy. He would have liked it like anything.—Especially when Francis Fran was backing away so-o-o quietly, and backed right into one of the Leopard-Men and had to run." She laughed again, "Daddy, are there really Leopard-Men on the Moon?"

"Probably not," said Weston absently. "It's just funny make-believe." He couldn't take much longer with the car. He'd have to face it.

Gloria ran across the lawn. "Robbie.—Robbie!"

Then she stopped suddenly at the sight of a beautiful collie which regarded her out of serious brown eyes as it wagged its tail on the porch.

"Oh, what a nice dog!" Gloria climbed the steps, approached cautiously and patted it. "Is it for me, Daddy?"

Her mother had joined them. "Yes, it is, Gloria. Isn't it nice—soft and furry. It's very gentle. It *likes* little girls."

"Can he play games?"

"Surely. He can do any number of tricks. Would you like to see some?"

"Right away. I want Robbie to see him, too.—*Robbie!*" She stopped, uncertainly, and frowned, "I'll bet he's just staying in his room because he's mad at me for not taking him to the visivox. You'll have to explain to him, Daddy. He might not believe me, but he knows if you say it, it's so."

Weston's lip grew tighter. He looked toward his wife but could not catch her eye.

Gloria turned precipitously and ran down the basement steps, shouting as she went, "Robbie—Come and see what Daddy and Mamma brought me. They brought me a dog, Robbie."

In a minute she had returned, a frightened little girl. "Mamma, Robbie isn't in his room. Where is he?" There was no answer and George Weston coughed and was suddenly extremely interested in an aimlessly drifting cloud. Gloria's voice quavered on the verge of tears, "Where's Robbie, Mamma?"

Mrs. Weston sat down and drew her daughter gently to her, "Don't feel bad, Gloria. Robbie has gone away, I think."

"Gone *away*? Where? Where's he gone away, Mamma?"

"No one knows, darling. He just walked away. We've looked and we've looked and we've looked for him, but we can't find him."

"You mean he'll never come back again?" Her eyes were round with horror.

"We may find him soon. We'll keep looking for him. And meanwhile you can play with your nice new doggie. Look at him! His name is Lightning and he can—"

But Gloria's eyelids had overflown, "I don't want the nasty dog—I want Robbie. I want you to find me Robbie." Her feelings became too deep for words, and she spluttered into a shrill wail.

Mrs. Weston glanced at her husband for help, but he merely shuffled his feet morosely and did not withdraw his ardent stare from the heavens, so she bent to the task of consolation, "Why do you cry, Gloria? Robbie was only a machine, just a nasty old machine. He wasn't alive at all."

"He was *not* no machine!" screamed Gloria, fiercely and ungrammatically. "He was a *person* just like you and me and he was my *friend*. I want him back. Oh, Mamma, I want him back."

Her mother groaned in defeat and left Gloria to her sorrow.

"Let her have her cry out," she told her husband. "Childish griefs are never lasting. In a few days, she'll forget that awful robot ever existed."

But time proved Mrs. Weston a bit too optimistic. To be sure, Gloria ceased crying, but she ceased smiling, too, and the passing days found her ever more silent and shadowy. Gradually, her attitude of passive unhappiness wore Mrs. Weston down and all that kept her from yielding was the impossibility of admitting defeat to her husband.

Then, one evening, she flounced into the living room, sat down, folded her arms and looked boiling mad.

Her husband stretched his neck in order to see her over his newspaper, "What now, Grace?"

"It's that child, George. I've had to send back the dog to-day. Gloria positively couldn't stand the sight of him, she said. She's driving me into a nervous breakdown."

Weston laid down the paper and a hopeful gleam entered his eye, "Maybe—Maybe we ought to get Robbie back. It might be done, you know. I can get in touch with—"

"No!" she replied, grimly. "I won't hear of it. We're not giving up that easily. My child shall *not* be brought up by a robot if it takes years to break her of it."

Weston picked up his paper again with a disappointed air. "A year of this will have me prematurely gray."

"You're a big help, George," was the frigid answer. "What Gloria needs is a change of environment. Of course she can't forget Robbie here. How can she when every tree and rock reminds her of him? It is really the *silliest*

situation I have ever heard of. Imagine a child pining
away for the loss of a robot."

"Well, stick to the point. What's the change in environment you're planning?"

"We're going to take her to New York."

"The city! In August! Say, do you know what New York
is like in August? It's unbearable."

"Millions do bear it."

"They don't have a place like this to go to. If they didn't
have to stay in New York, they wouldn't."

"Well, *we* have to. I say we're leaving now—or as soon
as we can make the arrangements. In the city, Gloria will
find sufficient interests and sufficient friends to perk her
up and make her forget that machine."

"Oh, Lord," groaned the lesser half, "those frying pave-
ments!"

"We have to," was the unshaken response. "Gloria has
lost five pounds in the last month and my little girl's
health is more important to me than your comfort."

"It's a pity you didn't think of your little girl's health before you deprived her of her pet robot," he muttered—but
to himself.

Gloria displayed immediate signs of improvement when
told of the impending trip to the city. She spoke little
of it, but when she did, it was always with lively anticipa-
tion. Again, she began to smile and to eat with something
of her former appetite.

Mrs. Weston hugged herself for joy and lost no opportu-
nity to triumph over her still skeptical husband.

"You see, George, she helps with the packing like a little
angel, and chatters away as if she hadn't a care in the
world. It's just as I told you—all we need do is substitute
other interests."

"Hmpph," was the skeptical response, "I hope so."

Preliminaries were gone through quickly. Arrangements were made for the preparation of their city home and a couple were engaged as housekeepers for the country home. When the day of the trip finally did come, Gloria was all but her old self again, and no mention of Robbie passed her lips at all.

In high good-humor the family took a taxi-gyro to the airport (Weston would have preferred using his own private 'gyro, but it was only a two-seater with no room for baggage) and entered the waiting liner.

"Come, Gloria," called Mrs. Weston. "I've saved you a seat near the window so you can watch the scenery."

Gloria trotted down the aisle cheerily, flattened her nose into a white oval against the thick clear glass, and watched with an intentness that increased as the sudden coughing of the motor drifted backward into the interior. She was too young to be frightened when the ground dropped away as if let through a trap-door and she herself suddenly became twice her usual weight, but not too young to be mightily interested. It wasn't until the ground had changed into a tiny patch-work quilt that she withdrew her nose, and faced her mother again.

"Will we soon be in the city, Mamma?" she asked, rubbing her chilled nose, and watching with interest as the patch of moisture which her breath had formed on the pane shrank slowly and vanished.

"In about half an hour, dear." Then, with just the faintest trace of anxiety, "Aren't you glad we're going? Don't you think you'll be very happy in the city with all the buildings and people and things to see? We'll go to the visivox every day and see shows and go to the circus and the beach and—"

"Yes, Mamma," was Gloria's unenthusiastic rejoinder.

The liner passed over a bank of clouds at the moment, and
Gloria was instantly absorbed in the usual spectacle of
clouds underneath one. Then they were over clear sky
again, and she turned to her mother with a sudden myste-
rious air of secret knowledge.

"*I* know why we're going to the city, Mamma."

"Do you?" Mrs. Weston was puzzled. "Why, dear?"

"You didn't tell me because you wanted it to be a surprise, but *I* know." For a moment, she was lost in admiration at her own acute penetration, and then she laughed
gaily. "We're going to New York so we can find Robbie,
aren't we?—With detectives."

The statement caught George Weston in the middle of a
drink of water, with disastrous results. There was a sort of
strangled gasp, a geyser of water, and then a bout of chok-
ing coughs. When all was over, he stood there, a red-faced,
water-drenched and very, very annoyed person.

Mrs. Weston maintained her composure, but when Gloria
repeated her question in a more anxious tone of voice, she
found her temper rather bent.

"Maybe," she retorted, tartly. "Now sit and be still, for
Heaven's sake."

New York City, 1998 A.D., was a paradise for the sight-
seer more than ever in its history. Gloria's parents
realized this and made the most of it.

On direct orders from his wife, George Weston arranged
to have his business take care of itself for a month or so,
in order to be free to spend the time in what he termed
"dissipating Gloria to the verge of ruin." Like everything
else Weston did, this was gone about in an efficient, thor-
ough, and business-like way. Before the month had passed,
nothing that could be done had not been done.

She was taken to the top of the half-mile tall Roosevelt

Building, to gaze down in awe upon the jagged panorama
of rooftops that blended far off in the fields of Long Island
and the flatlands of New Jersey. They visited the zoos
where Gloria stared in delicious fright at the "real live
lion" (rather disappointed that the keepers fed him raw
steaks, instead of human beings, as she had expected), and
asked insistently and peremptorily to see "the whale."

The various museums came in for their share of attention, together with the parks and the beaches and the
aquarium.

She was taken halfway up the Hudson in an excursion
steamer fitted out in the archaism of the mad Twenties.
She travelled into the stratosphere on an exhibition trip,
where the sky turned deep purple and the stars came out
and the misty earth below looked like a huge concave
bowl. Down under the waters of the Long Island Sound she
was taken in a glass-walled sub-sea vessel, where in a

green and wavering world, quaint and curious sea-things ogled her and wiggled suddenly away.

On a more prosaic level, Mrs. Weston took her to the department stores where she could revel in another type of fairyland.

In fact, when the month had nearly sped, the Westons were convinced that everything conceivable had been done to take Gloria's mind once and for all off the departed Robbie—but they were not quite sure they had succeeded.

The fact remained that wherever Gloria went, she displayed the most absorbed and concentrated interest in such robots as happened to be present. No matter how exciting the spectacle before her, nor how novel to her girlish eyes, she turned away instantly if the corner of her eye caught a glimpse of metallic movement.

Mrs. Weston went out of her way to keep Gloria away from all robots.

And the matter was finally climaxed in the episode at the Museum of Science and Industry. The Museum had announced a special "children's program" in which exhibits of scientific witchery scaled down to the child mind were to be shown. The Westons, of course, placed it upon their list of "absolutely."

It was while the Westons were standing totally absorbed in the exploits of a powerful electro-magnet that Mrs. Weston suddenly became aware of the fact that Gloria was no longer with her. Initial panic gave way to calm decision and, enlisting the aid of three attendants, a careful search was begun.

Gloria, of course, was not one to wander aimlessly, however. For her age, she was an unusually determined and purposeful girl, quite full of the maternal genes in that respect. She had seen a huge sign on the third floor, which had said, "This Way to the Talking Robot." Having spelled it out to herself and having noticed that her parents did not seem to wish to move in the proper direction, she did the obvious thing. Waiting for an opportune moment of parental distraction, she calmly disengaged herself and followed the sign.

The Talking Robot was a *tour de force*, a thoroughly impractical device, possessing publicity value only. Once an hour, an escorted group stood before it and asked questions of the robot engineer in charge in careful whispers. Those the engineer decided were suitable for the robot's circuits were transmitted to the Talking Robot.

It was rather dull. It may be nice to know that the square of fourteen is one hundred ninety-six, that the temperature at the moment is 72 degrees Fahrenheit, and the air-pressure 30.02 inches of mercury, that the atomic weight of sodium is 23, but one doesn't really need a robot for that. One especially does not need an unwieldy, totally immobile mass of wires and coils spreading over twenty-five square yards.

Few people bothered to return for a second helping, but one girl in her middle teens sat quietly on a bench waiting for a third. She was the only one in the room when Gloria entered.

Gloria did not look at her. To her at the moment, another human being was but an inconsiderable item. She saved her attention for this large thing with the wheels. For a moment, she hesitated in dismay. It didn't look like any robot she had ever seen.

Cautiously and doubtfully she raised her treble voice, "Please, Mr. Robot, sir, are you the Talking Robot, sir?" She wasn't sure, but it seemed to her that a robot that actually talked was worth a great deal of politeness.

(The girl in her mid-teens allowed a look of intense concentration to cross her thin, plain face. She whipped out a small notebook and began writing in rapid pot-hooks.)

There was an oily whir of gears and a mechanically-timbred voice boomed out in words that lacked accent and intonation, "I—am—the—robot—that—talks."

Gloria stared at it ruefully. It *did* talk, but the sound came from inside somewheres. There was no *face* to talk to. She said, "Can you help me, Mr. Robot, sir?"

The Talking Robot was designed to answer questions, and only such questions as it could answer had ever been put to it. It was quite confident of its ability, therefore, "I—can—help—you."

"Thank you, Mr. Robot, sir. Have you seen Robbie?"

"Who—is Robbie?"

"He's a robot, Mr. Robot, sir." She stretched to tip-toes. "He's about so high, Mr. Robot, sir, only higher, and he's very nice. He's got a head, you know. I mean you haven't, but he has, Mr. Robot, sir."

The Talking Robot had been left behind, "A—robot?"

"Yes, Mr. Robot, sir. A robot just like you, except he can't talk, of course, and—looks like a real person."

"A—robot—like—me?"

"Yes, Mr. Robot, sir."

To which the Talking Robot's only response was an erratic splutter and an occasional incoherent sound. The radical generalization offered it, i.e., its existence, not as a particular object, but as a member of a general group, was too much for it. Loyally, it tried to encompass the concept and half a dozen coils burnt out. Little warning signals were buzzing.

(The girl in her mid-teens left at that point. She had enough for her Physics-1 paper on "Practical Aspects of Robotics." This paper was Susan Calvin's first of many on the subject.)

Gloria stood waiting, with carefully concealed impatience, for the machine's answer when she heard the cry behind her of "There she is," and recognized that cry as her mother's.

"What are you doing here, you bad girl?" cried Mrs. Weston, anxiety dissolving at once into anger. "Do you know you frightened your mamma and daddy almost to death? Why did you run away?"

The robot engineer had also dashed in, tearing his hair, and demanding who of the gathering crowd had tampered with the machine. "Can't anybody read signs?" he yelled. "You're not allowed in here without an attendant."

Gloria raised her grieved voice over the din, "I only came to see the Talking Robot, Mamma. I though he might know where Robbie was because they're both robots." And then, as the thought of Robbie was suddenly brought forcefully home to her, she burst into a sudden storm of tears, "And I *got* to find Robbie, Mamma. I *got* to."

Mrs. Weston strangled a cry, and said, "Oh, good Heavens. Come home, George. This is more than I can stand."

That evening, George Weston left for several hours, and the next morning, he approached his wife with something that looked suspiciously like smug complacence.

"I've got an idea, Grace."

"About what?" was the gloomy, uninterested query.

"About Gloria."

"You're not going to suggest buying back that robot?"

"No, of course not."

"Then go ahead. I might as well listen to you. Nothing *I've* done seems to have done any good."

"All right. Here's what I've been thinking. The whole trouble with Gloria is that she thinks of Robbie as a *person* and not as a *machine*. Naturally, she can't forget him. Now if we managed to convince her that Robbie was nothing more than a mess of steel and copper in the form of sheets and wires with electricity its juice of life, how long would her longings last? It's the psychological attack, if you see my point."

"How do you plan to do it?"

"Simple. Where do you suppose I went last night? I persuaded Robertson of U. S. Robots and Mechanical Men, Inc. to arrange for a complete tour of his premises tomorrow. The three of us will go, and by the time we're through, Gloria will have it drilled into her that a robot is *not* alive."

Mrs. Weston's eyes widened gradually and something glinted in her eyes that was quite like sudden admiration, "Why, George, that's a *good* idea."

And George Weston's vest buttons strained. "Only kind I have," he said.

Mr. Struthers was a conscientious General Manager and naturally inclined to be a bit talkative. The combination, therefore, resulted in a tour that was fully explained, perhaps even over-abundantly explained, at every step. However, Mrs. Weston was not bored. Indeed, she stopped him several times and begged him to repeat his statements in simpler language so that Gloria might understand. Under the influence of this appreciation of his narrative powers,

Mr. Struthers expanded genially and became ever more communicative, if possible.

George Weston, himself, showed a gathering impatience.

"Pardon me, Struthers," he said, breaking into the middle of a lecture on the photo-electric cell, "haven't you a section of the factory where only robot labor is employed?"

"Eh? Oh, yes! Yes, indeed!" He smiled at Mrs. Weston. "A vicious circle in a way, robots creating more robots. Of course, we are not making a general practice out of it. For one thing, the unions would never let us. But we can turn out a very few robots using robot labor exclusively, merely as a sort of scientific experiment. You see," he tapped his pince-nez into one palm argumentatively, "what the labor unions don't realize—and I say this as a man who has always been very sympathetic with the labor movement in general—is that the advent of the robot, while involving some dislocation to begin with, will inevitably—"

"Yes, Struthers," said Weston, "but about that section of the factory you speak of—may we see it? It would be very interesting, I'm sure."

"Yes! Yes, of course!" Mr. Struthers replaced his pince-nez in one convulsive movement and gave vent to a soft cough of discomfiture. "Follow me, please."

He was comparatively quiet while leading the three through a long corridor and down a flight of stairs. Then, when they had entered a large well-lit room that buzzed with metallic activity, the sluices opened and the flood of explanation poured forth again.

"There you are!" he said with pride in his voice. "Robots only! Five men act as overseers and they don't even stay in this room. In five years, that is, since we began this project, not a single accident has occurred. Of course, the robots here assembled are comparatively simple, but . . ."

The General Manager's voice had long died to a rather

soothing murmur in Gloria's ears. The whole trip seemed rather dull and pointless to her, though there *were* many robots in sight. None were even remotely like Robbie, though, and she surveyed them with open contempt.

In this room, there weren't any people at all, she noticed. Then her eyes fell upon six or seven robots busily engaged at a round table halfway across the room. They widened in incredulous surprise. It was a big room. She couldn't see for sure, but one of the robots looked like— looked like—*it was!*

"*Robbie!*" Her shriek pierced the air, and one of the robots about the table faltered and dropped the tool he was holding. Gloria went almost mad with joy. Squeezing through the railing before either parent could stop her, she dropped lightly to the floor a few feet below, and ran toward her Robbie, arms waving and hair flying.

And the three horrified adults, as they stood frozen in their tracks, saw what the excited little girl did not see,— a huge, lumbering tractor bearing blindly down upon its appointed track.

It took split-seconds for Weston to come to his senses, and those split-seconds meant everything, for Gloria could not be overtaken. Although Weston vaulted the railing in a wild attempt, it was obviously hopeless. Mr. Struthers signalled wildly to the overseers to stop the tractor, but the overseers were only human and it took time to act.

It was only Robbie that acted immediately and with precision.

With metal legs eating up the space between himself and his little mistress he charged down from the opposite direction. Everything then happened at once. With one sweep of an arm, Robbie snatched up Gloria, slackening his speed not one iota, and, consequently, knocking every breath of air out of her. Weston, not quite comprehending all that

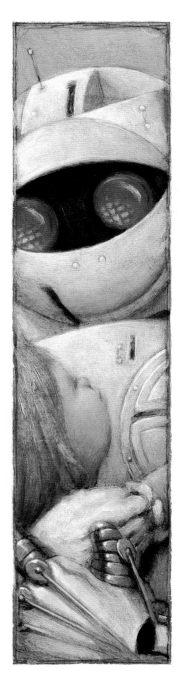

was happening, felt, rather than saw, Robbie brush past him, and came to a sudden bewildered halt. The tractor intersected Gloria's path half a second after Robbie had, rolled on ten feet further and came to a grinding, long drawn-out stop.

Gloria regained her breath, submitted to a series of passionate hugs on the part of both her parents and turned eagerly toward Robbie. As far as she was concerned, nothing had happened except that she had found her friend.

But Mrs. Weston's expression had changed from one of relief to one of dark suspicion. She turned to her husband, and, despite her disheveled and undignified appearance, managed to look quite formidable, "*You* engineered this, *didn't* you?"

George Weston swabbed at a hot forehead with his handkerchief. His hand was unsteady, and his lips could curve only into a tremulous and exceedingly weak smile.

Mrs. Weston pursued the thought, "Robbie wasn't designed for engineering or construction work. He couldn't be of any use to them. You had him placed there deliberately so that Gloria would find him. You know you did."

"Well, I did," said Weston. "But, Grace, how was I to know the reunion would be so violent? And Robbie has saved her life; you'll have to admit that. You *can't* send him away again."

Grace Weston considered. She turned toward Gloria and Robbie and watched them abstractedly for a moment. Gloria had a grip about the robot's neck that would have asphyxiated any creature but one of metal, and was prattling nonsense in half-hysterical frenzy. Robbie's chrome-steel arms (capable of bending a bar of steel two inches in diameter into a pretzel) wound about the little girl gently and lovingly, and his eyes glowed a deep, deep red.

"Well," said Mrs. Weston, at last, "I guess he can stay with us until he rusts."

o   o   o

About the Author

Little did Judah and Anna Asimov know, in 1923, when they immigrated to the United States from Russia, that their son, Isaac, would become one of the most prolific and respected writers of our time. When the Asimov family arrived in the United States, they settled in Brooklyn, where they opened a candy store.

At the age of nine, Isaac began working in his parents' store after school. It was then he discovered the magic inside the science fiction magazines which the candy store sold. Being very strict, Isaac's father only consented to Isaac reading these magazines because he believed they were about science, and he wanted his son to one day be a doctor.

Being an excellent student, Isaac graduated from high school when he was only fifteen years old. He went directly on to Columbia University where he chose chemistry as his pre-med course of study. Asimov's interest in writing had been building for many years, and he was excited when he sold his first science fiction story while still in college. After graduation, he went on to obtain his M.A. in chemistry from Columbia before serving as a Naval chemist in World War II. Asimov returned from the war and began working on his Ph.D., also in chemistry from Columbia University, which he finished in 1948. Asimov had continued writing science fiction this whole time when, in 1949, he was asked to teach biochemistry at Boston University. Enjoying teaching and lecturing very much, Asimov accepted the position.

Asimov continued to write during his tenure at the university, but found it increasingly difficult to spend the necessary time on his writing and teaching. In 1958, Asimov decided to leave Boston Uni-

versity and devote himself to writing full-time. By then, Asimov had broadened his writing to include non-fiction, and he was developing a reputation for being a standout author of science texts for young people and laymen. He has continued, since that time, to produce a vast body of material which ranges from science fiction, to science fact, to history to Shakespeare. When asked how he could possibly write on so many diverse subjects, Asimov explained that his purpose is not to become an expert on any one thing, but rather, to learn what is necessary of a topic to discuss it intelligently.

One area in which Asimov is universally considered expert is robotics. Asimov developed, in his 1959 novel, I, ROBOT, the three laws of robotics. They are: (1) A robot may not injure a human being, or through inaction allow a human being to come to harm, (2) a robot must obey the orders given it by human beings except where such orders would conflict with the first law, and (3) a robot must protect its own existence as long as such protection does not conflict with the first or second law. Although written nearly forty years ago, it is believed these laws will be incorporated into robots of the future.

Asimov has also established himself as a first-rate lecturer. He enjoys it very much and lectures frequently on the East coast. Asimov considers himself a "ham" and can speak for hours in front of a responsive audience.

In the past, in the present, and most certainly in the future, Isaac Asimov is a name which is widely known and highly respected. It is a name which graces many literary genres and lecture halls. It is a name which represents a man who can, above all, communicate on many levels, about many things, with many people.

About the Artist

David Shannon graduated from Art Center College of Design in 1983 and now lives in New York City. His work has appeared in many publications including Time, The New York Times, *and* Rolling Stone, *as well as on a poster for a Broadway play.*

ART DIRECTION AND DESIGN
Tilman Reitzle

COLOR SEPARATIONS
Colour Graphics—Minneapolis, Minnesota

BIOGRAPHY
Cindy Fitterer Klingel

TYPESETTING
Trufont Typographers, Inc.—Hicksville, New York

PRINTING
Worzalla Publishing Co.—Stevens Point, Wisconsin

ALSO BY
ISAAC ASIMOV

Sally

All the Troubles of the World

Franchise

It's Such a Beautiful Day

Published by Creative Education